POCKET · PUFFINS

For Phil

Puffin Books, Penguin Books Ltd, Harmondsworth, Middlesex, England
Viking Penguin Inc., 40 West 23rd Street, New York, New York 10010, U.S.A.
Penguin Books Australia Ltd, Ringwood, Victoria, Australia
Penguin Books Canada Limited, 2801 John Street, Markham, Ontario, Canada L3R 1B4
Penguin Books (N.Z.) Ltd, 182-190 Wairau Road, Auckland 10, New Zealand

Puffin/Moonlight
First published in the United Kingdom by William Collins Sons & Co. Ltd 1981
Text and illustrations copyright © Irene Haas, 1981
Published in Pocket Puffins 1987 in association with Moonlight Publishing Ltd,
131 Kensington Church Street, London W8

Printed in Italy by La Editoriale Libraria

The Little Moon Theatre

by Irene Haas

POCKET  PUFFINS

Jo Jo, Jip and Nicolette were a troupe of travelling players. They rode through the countryside giving performances every night in a different place. Whenever they came into a new village, Jip would bang the drum and blow the horn, Nicolette danced to the beat of her tambourine and Jo Jo would sing this song:

When supper is over tonight,
walk out in the evening light.
Come to the theatre,
The Little Moon Theatre,
come to the theatre tonight.

Don't put the baby to bed,
put a cap on its fuzzy round head
and come to the theatre,
The Little Moon Theatre,
come to the theatre instead.

Day is done, nothing to do,
so Baby and Mama and you
all come to the theatre,
The Little Moon Theatre,
and bring us a penny or two!"

One fine spring afternoon, Jo Jo drove the caravan into the middle of a sleepy little village. People on their way home to supper stopped and listened to her song, and suddenly the village was wide awake

with excitement. The villagers hurried to eat supper and dress in their best so they could walk out in the evening light to the theatre.

Jo Jo, Jip and Nicolette rode through the now-empty streets, looking for a good place to give the show. They were close to the edge of town when they turned a

corner and found a little girl sitting on the kerb crying. They stopped.

"My name is Rose, and I like to wear a red sock on this foot," the little girl explained, "and a yellow sock on this foot, but my mother says that's contrary and that I can't come to the show tonight."

"Aha," said Jo Jo, "but did your mother say you can't be *in* the show tonight? Come aboard The Little Moon, Rose!"

The little girl climbed up and sat next to Nicolette.
"I *wish* my mother wouldn't mind my socks," she whispered.

That night the play was called *The Wise Prince*. Jo Jo plucked her guitar and told this story:

Once long ago, a prince had to choose between two beautiful maidens. One would be the queen. He gave them each two tests, one in dancing and one in singing.

The music began and the first maiden did a toe dance with long leaps and difficult twirls. The second maiden decided to do something different, so she took a silken cord from the castle curtains and jumped rope with it, fast and fancy.

Then it was time to sing. The first maiden went to the centre of the stage and sang a beautiful old song with many verses. It began:

> *I dreamt that I dwelt*
> *In marble halls,*
> *With vassals and serfs*
> *at my side.*

The second maiden decided to do something different so she sang:

Three little nincompoops
sitting in a tree.
Their names were
Do and Re and Me.
Do and Re
fell out of the tree,
so who was left?

"Oh, I know that," cried the first maiden. "It's ME!"

Then Jo Jo sang:
> *The prince chose Rose.*
> *He liked her socks, you see.*
> *He knew that it was special*
> *to do things differently.*

The prince chose Rose.
He kissed her hand and said
he'd wear his socks
the way she did,
one yellow and one red!

The play was over. The actors bowed while the audience applauded and tossed flowers to the stage for Rose. She gazed into the crowd of faces and saw her mother smiling proudly. Soon the villagers went home, feeling sleepy and contented. Rose and her mother walked hand in hand.

When the costumes had been put away, the scenery rolled up and the coins counted, Jo Jo, Jip and Nicolette settled down to a late supper. Jo Jo dished out big plates of simmering stew. Suddenly, something fell from out of the sky and splashed into the river! Jip swam out

quickly and brought a little shivering bundle back to shore.

It was a tiny old woman, an old fairy godmother. Her wings were weak with weariness.

"I've one wish left in my old magic wand," she whispered, "and when it is granted I can rest."

"Who will have the last wish?" asked Jo Jo.

"It's for a child I cannot find. She wears one yellow sock and one red sock and wishes that her mother wouldn't mind."

"Oh, Madam!" said Jo Jo. "The Little Moon Travelling Theatre made that wish come true, so you still have one wish left to do."

The little old woman shivered more than ever. They warmed her and fed her and put her to bed.
In the morning she flew off once more and the troupe packed up to go, to another village and another show.

On a day in midsummer, The Little Moon Travelling Theatre, journeying through green valleys and hills, found a little boy sitting all alone on a bridge. He held something in his arms. "I'm here all alone," he said, "because people are afraid of my snake. I *wish* they could see how beautiful he is and how good."

Jo Jo invited him aboard and they all rode into the next village.

That night the play was called *Hero of the Jungle*. The curtains parted. Jip and Nicolette appeared wearing strange animal masks.

Night had fallen in the jungle; and Jo Jo sang this story-song:

'Twas the night
of the animal fair.
The birds and the beasts
would be there
The old baboon
by the light of the moon
was combing
his auburn hair.

But the jungle was
full of dread,
for the crocodile,
it was said,
was eating great feasts
of the smallest beasts.
Imagine the tears
that were shed!

You could hear
the crocodile roar
as she searched in
her dresser drawer.
'I'll look like a fool
if I don't have a jewel
to dress up my pinafore!'

Now a handsome young
snake, he strayed
to the crocodile
place, unafraid.
'Please let me bedeck
your magnificent neck
like a necklace
of lapis and jade!'

The birds and the beasts
that night
cheered the snake
with all of their might,
for the crocodile swore
she'd eat beasties

no more
if her necklace
stopped
squeezing
so tight!

When the play was over the snake was truly a hero. The boy walked home with the snake on his shoulders, while the villagers followed, admiring its goodness and beauty.

Later that night, as Jo Jo, Jip and
Nicolette worked and listened to the song
of the summer crickets, they heard
another sad little sound. Nicolette dashed
up a tree and found the little old fairy
godmother dangling from a branch by her
pocketbook strap. As Nicolette carried her

gently down, the tiny woman whispered, "My worn old wings are so weary, but I've one last wish in my old magic wand and when it is granted I can rest."

"Who will have the last wish?" asked Jo Jo.

"I looked for a boy, before my fall, who wished that folks liked his snake, that's all."

"Oh, Madam!" said Jo Jo. "Tonight we made that wish come true, so you still have one wish left to do."

The tiny old woman was warmed, fed and put to bed.

In the morning she flew off once more and the troupe packed up to go, to another village and another show.

On an evening in autumn, The Little Moon Travelling Theatre, journeying through a landscape of red and gold, saw a hound dog on top of a hill, howling sadly. "My heart is breaking," he told them.

"I can't do my work, which is chasing raccoon. All I can do is *wish* for the moon!" So they took him aboard and as they rode together into the next village the great pink sun disappeared.

The play that night was called *The Dog Who Loved the Moon*. This was the dog's song:

Can I win the moon
with a rapturous tune?
If I howl and I croon
like a loon to the moon,
will she come to me soon?
If I weep and I swoon,
will she hear me, the moon?

This was the moon's song:

> *Oh, little earth dog,*
> *dear loving clown,*
> *I'm not made of*
> *silver or pearl*
> *or marble or ice*
> *or anything nice,*
> *and I'll never, no never*
> *come down.*

But I have little sisters,
(don't weep!)
tiny copies of me everywhere.
They are not way up high
in the star-dappled sky.
So take this one
to love and to keep.

Nicolette gave him the little moon from the roof of the caravan.

When the play was over, Jo Jo, Jip and Nicolette watched as the hound hurried home, holding his moon tenderly in his teeth.

The night was chilly, and when a great gust of wind blew by, it carried the fairy godmother, helpless, over their heads. Jo Jo ran and jumped and pulled her down. They took the little old woman into the caravan behind the stage and the painted scenery. It was warm there and supper was cooking.

"Oh my worn old wings are so weary," cried the tiny woman, "but I've one last wish in my old magic wand and when it is granted I can rest."

"Who will have the last wish?" asked Jo Jo.

"I looked for a dog who wished for the moon, but my poor old wings gave out too soon."

"Oh, Madam!" said Jo Jo. "Tonight we made that wish come true, so you still have one wish left to do."

The old woman was warmed, fed and put to bed. In the morning she flew off once more and the troupe packed up to go, to another village and another show.

And then it was winter. Jo Jo played her violin, her fingers stiff with cold. Snowflakes fell on Jip and Nicolette as they danced, watched only by a family of white wolves and an old snowy owl.

"How I *wish* we could be warm," whispered Jo Jo.

Later that night they heard a strange noise, and they rushed outside to see what it was. The tiny old fairy godmother had just fallen from the sky into the deep snow. As they lifted her out she cried, "At last!" and she raised her magic wand.

"This is warm sand between my toes," said Jo Jo, "and warm sun upon my nose!"

Nicolette and Jip lifted their heads. They smelled jacaranda and ilang-ilang flowers in the soft warm breeze.

"No freezing winds, no winter snows?
How did we get here, do you suppose?"
asked Jo Jo.

And the little old fairy godmother, in her old striped bathing suit, dipped and dunked her tiny body in the aquamarine sea and smiled.

Hello, I'm Smudge

Would you like to hear about my book club?

It's for 4-8 year-olds and you get your own badge, membership book and a Club magazine four times a year.

It's packed with stories, puzzles and competitions.

You get a chance to buy new books!

And there's lots more! For further details and an application form send a stamped, addressed envelope to:

The Junior Puffin Club,
P. O. Box 21,
Cranleigh,
Surrey,
GU6 8UZ